# Monarch.

By: Leah Maurizio

HAPPY Pride ♥
Hope you enjoy
the read ♥

Leah Maurizio

# Note To Reader

      I'm offering this volume of poetry to those of you that may have been so lucky to find your person. Lesbian women in particular, I hope my poetry speaks to you and the love you have been so lucky to experience. Although a few of the poems are directly personalized, allow my quest in manifesting my wife to express your devotion to the woman you are set to marry. In fact, gift this to her on your wedding day, as I intend to do so to my wife on our wedding day.

I hope you resonate with these pages and that my book ties you closer to your partner.

Thank you,

Leah

# Dedication

To my wife,

If this book should find you before I do, I hope it ignites your soul on its journey to mine. I absolutely cannot wait to love you. And if by chance I was blessed enough to hand it to you first, this is my promise and devotion to you. Either way, it has been a long and hard journey to get to you.

I am manifesting you with these pages and aim to keep you with their promises.

You are my absolute favorite everything.

I love you.

## To My Person

I want to love you.
  Even when it doesn't feel so good,
I want to love you.

I want to see you.
  Even when I'm seeing someone I
haven't seen before,
I want to see you.

I want to hold you in these moments
  And also set you free.

I want you to fly next to me and
  Away from me, but always make
Your way back home;

I want to love you.

No, I don't want to keep you,
  I want to love you.
No, I don't want to cage you,
  I want to love you.

And I want to see you
  And feel you
And hold you
  And kiss you in the places you
Feel the most joy and the most pain

I want to love you.
  Will you let me love you?

## Sunday

Sunday came and went,
  Another week has gone by,
And I wonder if that means
  I'm another week closer to you.

I looked for you in the crowd,
  I always do.
I'd be lying if I said I didn't
  Because how don't you
Keep an eye out for your person?

Are you her?
  Is she you?
I wonder.

Maybe I'll see you Sunday?

## You and the Moon

I listen for your name when the wind
  Blows through my hair,
Sending soft whispers to my ear
  And a chill down my spine,
As your hands and lips someday will.

The sun pressed against my skin,
  Foreshadowing the warmth of you in
the morning,
Curled up into every piece of me.

How is it that I can feel you
  All around me,
Getting closer and closer each day,
  Knowing we are staring at the same
moon,
But I do not know you yet?

Do I know you yet?
  Do you feel me too?

Tonight let's both talk to the moon.

## Celestial

Heaven can't be a place too far away
  Because the bliss that is us
When we are skin to skin
  Has to touch down from
Somewhere celestial.

And when I'm with you,
  I see angel numbers near and
All around me, and I swear
  They have to be engraved in your skin
Because you can't tell me
  They didn't guide me here...

You are perfectly orchestrated,
  All of your lines divine,
And I swear I see the stars in your eyes.

You can't tell me the universe didn't
  Create us as one.

## Simple and Sweet

I hope we always find our way back
  To the beginning
When looking at one another felt
  Like a dream
And learning one another felt like
  Reading the most intense, beautiful
story.

I hope we find ourselves there
  After 20 years, looking over at one
Another on a porch swing thinking,
  "Wow, we really did it, didn't we?"

I hope we always find our way back
  To simple and sweet.

Let's keep this simple and sweet.

## The Universe & You

When our tongues intertwine,
  It's like I can feel the universe
Between our lips.

Tasting you is seamless,
  No beginning or resolution;
Because I simply cannot get enough
  And I'm unsure of where
I end and you begin.

We aren't here when
  We are skin to skin.

I swear our souls go off somewhere,

Somewhere between the universe and
you.

## Bed Sheets

Right now, life is very single.
  I spend most of my days alone,
Loving me wholeheartedly,
  Until one day,
You come take some of that weight.

I dream of you,
  But I don't move much while I sleep.
This king bed feels extra big without you,
  As I hardly touch your side.

I'm sick of folding back
  One corner each morning
And placing back one set of pillows,
  As yours stay perfectly propped,
Awaiting your dreams and arrival.

This bed's too easy to make.

I can't wait to fix your side,
  Knowing you were well-rested
In these sheets.

Nothing is Forever

Every time I meet someone new,
    I look for you in their eyes.

See, I have this idea that
    I'll be able to know if it's you
Looking back at me,

And when they touch my skin,
    I pay close attention to if
Their hands were made for touching me
    Because something tells me
I'll know when it's you.

So far, I haven't found you in any of
them.
    I was fooled into thinking so once or
twice,
But nothing is forever, right?

If anything is,
    I know it's you.

## Etched in Skin

Every time one of the others broke my
heart,
   I dove into my canvas
And let the needle heal my wounds
   As it created another.

One day, as you trace my skin,
   You'll gaze at the illustrations
While I tell you my story.

See, there are tiny pieces of past lovers
   Etched in my skin
And their scars have added character to
   A once blank canvas.

These are the scars that have made me
into art.

I did something crazy after my last
heartbreak
   And I got a tattoo for you.

It's in the center of my chest,
   Waiting for you to uncover.

You'll see it and understand it
   As you love my layers...

It's my favorite page of the story,
   I'll read it to you over and over.

## Their Favorites

I would ask them about themselves,
　Paying close attention to every detail
so
I knew exactly how to make them smile.

I'd learn how to cook their favorite
meals,
　How they liked their clothes folded,
How to help them unwind at night
　After a long day.

I'd set out their towels and PJs
　For after their shower and play
With their hair until that and
　My heartbeat put them to sleep
As I finished watching their favorite
shows.

I'd do all of this with a glimmer in my
eye;
　I was so in love,
They never were.

I knew all their favorites
　And they still chose someone new.

Not you though,
　You never would.

## The Giving Tree

I was growing,
  Fresh, youthful
And so much heart to give.

My hands constantly offering it out
  On a silver platter
Thinking they would love what they see
  And keep it safe.

They didn't.
  But, I still gave and gave
As my brightest parts wilted
  And they left me with just
Branches of skin and bone
  And a very hollow chest.

And then, I'd water myself again
  While the sun shined down on me,
Bringing back all of my brightest parts,
  And I'd grow.

Until another needed what I had
  And I was a fool to give,
But I gave.

I hope this is the last time I'll have to
grow
  Because you will get all I have left to
give.

## Decompose

I want the thread that binds us
  To keep us as close as skin,
For now that I know your flesh,
  I want ours bound as one,
Hand-in-hand
  Until our fingers decompose.

## Extraterrestrial

The places we take one another
  As our tongues intertwine
Reach heights I'm convinced
  No one else has gone.

You reach deep inside of me,
  Making every part of my existence
yours,
Taking me somewhere extraterrestrial,
  As my soul drips down your palms.

## Light

The way the sun shines
  Down on your facial structure in the
morning
As you sleep so peacefully
  Creates a dreamy aura,
Putting me into a daze.

Most dawns do not feel real
  Because how is something
I longed deeply for
  Angelically existing right before my
eyes?

You and the light within me
  Were created as one so very long ago,
And oh how my half missed yours
  During the journey back to one
another.

## Unison

It's in the way our hearts found a way
   To beat as one.
The syncopation creates music
   Only we can understand,
But I swear others can hear it
   While in our presence.

Two bodies with two heartbeats
   Taking two separate breaths,
Yet in unison.

You and I are meant to ebb and flow,
   Effortlessly fluctuating
To design and sustain a sole being.

## Tides

Rising, falling
  My chest fully controlled by you.

You're so pretty,
  Brightly existing in all your glory,
Standing alone perfectly.

You are to be nothing but admired.

Like the moon...
  To the tides,
You are to I.

And, I'm just happy to be so loved by you
  That you chose to exist in my sky.

## Blurred Image

I've always been able to see you,
  You have been within my mind for as
long as I can remember.
The most beautiful, blurred image that I
so badly wish I could
  See better if I just squinted my eyes,
But then I'd know you too soon
  And there would be no dreaming or grit
to get to you.
So, I settle for your white aura
  And follow you through my thoughts.

Quiet

Consumed by rumination and trauma,
  My mind seems to know how to do
everything
But stop.

Then, I feel your palm press against
  The back of my neck,
Pulling us nose to nose.

And suddenly,
  My world is quiet.

## Your Voice

From when you are laughing with
　　Tears in your eyes,
To coming to me with the same for
warmth,
　　To gripping my shoulder blades...
I will never get over your voice
　　Saying my name.

<u>To Have and to Hold</u>

What a wild journey it will be
　To have held your hand,
Once smooth, interlocked within mine,
　To wilted and our fingers softly laced
together.

Timeless

They say that if you fall in love with
someone's eyes,
 You will be in love forever.

I've been in love with yours since the day
we met.

Timeless
 Ageless
Vessels to the soul

I find you there every time,
 And I will continually fall in love
Until they close for eternal rest.

Half-Loved

I was so used to loving enough for
    The both of us
Until you came along.

I was always half-loved,
    So naturally I filled the space
On my own,
    Hoping they would stay.

You love me fully,
    There's no space to fill.

We collide at a center
    I never knew existed,
Where love is fully balanced
    And leaving isn't even a thought.

## Self Love

I spent so much time
  Picking up what was left of me
When they walked out.

I built my being
  Time and time again
And loved myself back together.

There was only so much
  I could heal alone.

I always wondered what would ease
  The ache of trauma that told me
Love is just a moment.

Your lips pressed against my forehead
  Close my eyes and
Hit like Novocain,
  Promising the truth is the opposite.

Cold Coffee

Brewing two cups instead of one
  Is one of my favorite simplicities of
Morning love.

Sleepy-eyed Sundays
  That are taken very slow,
Until we sit over cold coffee.

## Monarch

I always felt you coming closer
  Each time the Monarch found me.

I'd acknowledge and smile
  As it danced around my energy field,
Making it known we were being
  Spiritually guided somewhere.

Even when it was hard,
  It knew how to make me smile
With its reassuring presence.

"She's out there, Le,
  Just follow me."

## Your Bones

It's chilling,
  Yet provides so much warmth.
Crippling to my absolute core,
  Yet is exactly what keeps my being
alive.

The way I love you
  Is the deepest, most immense creation,
And I truly cannot put it into words.

There is not enough ink,
  Not enough paper to express it.

I love you
  Deeply, madly, truly,
Down to your bones.

## Repurposed

Only your eyes could see me
  As you do.

They glisten when you look at me,
  No matter the circumstance.

There is so much love in your eyes.

All for this burned, battered,
  Repurposed skin.

But, it is seasoned and
  It is wise.
It has your name engraved through all
its layers,

Like an antique,
  Well used and at its fate,
Yet you still found beauty in it;

And now,
  All yours.

## Ring Finger

Did you know that
  Your ring finger applies the least amount
Of pressure amongst the five?

I suppose it is so because
  Once our souls are bound as one,
It carries the weight
  Of that very symbol.

Your ring looks absolutely beautiful on you,
  My love,

And you know you have me
  Wrapped around that
Pretty little finger.

## A Closeness

How do you do that?

Touch me in a way that
    Stirs me to my core.
Where there was once an absence,
    There is now feeling...

How?

I'm pulled into a
    Whirlwind of you,
And I wouldn't want out if you let me.

For as long as we live,
    A closeness I will always desire and
never forget.

Time

I am fully devoted to you
  For as long as our flesh
Is granted in manmade time.

But, I have loved you long before
  And will love you far beyond.

I love you within the gaps
  Between the smallest increments
And even more through the largest.

You were mine
  In many lives before this one,
And you will be mine in any to come.

I promise to always find you
  In every lifetime.

## Stardust

It's hard to fathom that
  Our connectivity is so strong
That our beings were so eager
  To exist at once.

Within the same universe,
  The same galaxy,
Amongst the same stardust,
  Birthed into the same planet
Of a mere solar system,

Just to be as one
  In the flesh of a human experience.

Every time my lips taste yours
  I flash back to that journey through the
stars
And I understand exactly why
  My soul needed to find yours.

## 1222

Angel number 1222,
  A sign of reunion
After being estranged.

The time is 12:22
  License plate LKH1222
Total: $12.22

I always knew it was guiding me to you.

It Doesn't Matter

It's funny how
  Our union erases the pain of the past.

We were never theirs
  And they were never ours.

We were just lost,
  Hoping through heartache,
Curled into those who came between...

But that is love
  And it doesn't matter because
You belong to me.

A Gift

And even after all this,
　I still know that you are
A gift,
　Not a given.

You will always be treated as such.

<u>I Believe You</u>

The abandonment wound
  Goes so deep, babe,
And I'm so sorry that
  You had to break through walls you
didn't build
And doors you didn't lock.

But, I thank you because
  I believe you.

<u>Eternity</u>

We are headed there,
   Yet we've been there...
Circling back as if
   One never happened
Before the other.
   Either way, it's you and I
Staring into eternity.

## Birthdays

Today is September 4, 2023.
  In one week, I turn 30.
I'm on my way back from a very special
trip;
  I celebrated with my mom.

I hope this is one year closer to you.
  I long for you.
I can't wait to spend the rest
  Of my birthdays with you, babe.

And of course I can't wait to celebrate
you;
  I'm so happy you exist.

## Marry Me

Not just this once,
  But a billion times over.

Every time we open our eyes,
  And when we are laid to rest.

Every single moment in between...
  Marry me,
Today and everyday?

## Fragrance

I love kissing behind your ear
  And nuzzling into your hair.

The smell of you is my favorite
fragrance;
  You smell of home and love and all
things beautiful.

It's euphoria I'll never get enough of.

I love you.

Road Maps

To grow old with you
　　Will be my biggest blessing.

I hope to still stare into your eyes
　　When they've aged and the wrinkles in
your skin
Display all the life you've lived
　　And places you've been.

I'll follow the lines in your flesh like
roadmaps,

Grazing upon their beauty
　　With my fingertips always leading me
home.

Reassurance

Don't you ever hesitate,
  Come running and
I'll be arms wide open.

Lean into me,
  Let me hold you through it and
Whisper every reassurance you need in
your ear
  And seal it with a kiss.

Don't you ever worry,
  It's you,
It's always been you,
  It'll only ever be you.

I'll never stop loving you.

Safe and Sound

I love when you fall asleep first,
  Head on my chest,
Little twitches,
  And then you nestle closer.

Safe and sound,
  I have my whole world in my arms,
Safe and sound.

## In the Clouds

I'm not going anywhere, baby.

If life gets way too hard,
    I'll meet you in the clouds.
We go there anyway, my love,
    And if that's too close to this crazy
place,
Then I'll meet you in the stars.
    It's prettier there anyways.
You'll never be alone.

## The Way You Move

You have the cutest way about you:
  The way your nose scrunches when
You smile bigger than your face,
  The way you dance around just to
make me laugh,
The way you hold your hands when
you're nervous...

I could kiss you 'til you're blue.

Your sleepy eyed smiles
  And silly slur when we've had too
much,

The rhythm we keep,
  The way you move
With me...

The perfect combination of sexy and
cute,

It's in everything you do.

## Bliss

The rush within my chest
  That you give me feels as if a billion
stars
Surround my heart.
  You are my perfectly imperfect.
This is bliss.

## My Wife

Your first and my last name
  Sound so good together.

My wife,

You wear it so well.

## Over My Dead Body

Giving up is not an option,
  Not here.
No towels will be thrown in,
  I will fight to the death to have you.
Give up?
  Over my dead body.

## I Want You

I want you.
   I do not need you,
But I want you.

My soul has always wanted yours,
   In every dimension,
It calls for you.

I want you,
   You and all your ugly,
Your flaws,
   Your deepest secrets,
Your demons,
   You and all your scars.

You are my version of perfect,
   I want you.

## Best Friend

It's my favorite thing you say next to,
  "I love you."

"Baby, you're my best friend."

You're mine too, gorgeous,
  You're my best friend,
My favorite friend,
  My truest friend.

For life, baby, for life.

## Slow

It's like a drip of molasses,
  Slow,
Deep,
  And so sweet.
You are so good.

Your hands grip my thighs
  And mine grip yours tighter,

Shaking,
  Melting into one another's curves.

You taste so good.

## Old

Don't you ever go,
   Just stay right here.

Darling, we may be old,
   But these souls are young.

I want to take my last breath with you.

Don't go before me,
   You mustn't.

We will go together,
   We always do.

But, if God calls us home differently,
   I will find you.

I will wait for you,
   And I will find you.

<u>4 Walls</u>

I'll never forget the nights that
  I longed for what I have now...

Someone to come home to.

I no longer come home to 4 walls
  Waiting for me.
I come home to the most beautiful and
warm spirit.

I get to come home to you,

Arms wide open,
  Eager to kiss me.

I was missed;
  You've been waiting for me.

## A Puzzle

I feel so understood by you.
   You love the way I love,
And you love me back the same.

The others couldn't comprehend me,
   I was far too complex for them,
A puzzle with pieces that could not
connect.

But you...

You sorted my pieces
   And carefully crafted each section of
My ever-loving soul until
   You saw me for the bigger picture that
I am.

And you fell in love,
   You called it art.

Dream

If you're wondering what it feels like
   To be in love with you,

It's as if you're having the same good
dream
   Over and over again.

I fall in love with you every single
second,
   And that's just the difference.

Pages

Simply put,
   I've just never experienced anything
quite like you.

Your hands tell my flesh stories,
   And I'll let you touch me enough to
Fill my pages.

## Slumber

I lay my head on your chest
  And fall to deep slumber.

Your heartbeat is my hymn.
  Your skin is my blanket.
Your arms hold my trust.

"Sleep, Darling.
  I'll be here in the morning."

## Museum

Crooked, cracked,
  Definitely bent out of shape, yet
Beautiful.

I am a battered work of art.

Once I realized this,
  I placed myself in my own museum
And allowed,
  Dared rather,
For someone to come stare at me long
enough
  And still want to take me home.

You took one good look
  And haven't let go of me since.

## Music

I hear your name
 While listening to music.

You should know you are cherished.

I always feel you at the place where
 Art and love collide.

Shall We?

Dance with me,
  Even if your feet stumble,

Allow me to hold you up
  As you rest your head on my shoulder.

We can sway in the kitchen
  To your favorite songs,

And I'll whisper sweet nothings
  In your ear
Until you feel like you again.

Take my hand,
  Shall we?

## A Choice

I choose you,
   I will always choose you.

Even in a thousand lifetimes,
   I would always choose us.

For as long as I'm breathing,
   I will keep choosing you.

See, love is a choice,
   But this is inevitable.

This love chose me many moons ago,

And in every phase it takes,
   I'm married to it more.

## Fantasy

When you touch me,
  My soul intertwines with yours
And leaves this world.

Wherever we go
  Is exactly where love resides,

And in that moment,
  I never want to open my eyes.

But when I do,
  I'm reminded that sometimes
Fantasy becomes reality,

And I no longer have to dream
  To feel you...

Your love is right here.

Surrender

I couldn't stop falling if I tried;

I lost all control and had to
    Surrender to the risk.

You were far too beautiful
    And love gleamed from your eyes.

So I fell,

And I keep on falling.

<u>Silence</u>

So many mornings
  I woke up to it.

Blessed to see another day,
  But so lonely.

Silence.

It was always waiting for me.

Waking up with the wrong one each
morning
  Until they left and well after.

But now, you.

You fill the space of dark and quiet,
  And even when there is not a sound to
be made,

I can still look over and count on you as
  We sit in silence.

Pieces

Sometimes I wish you had met me
   Before I went numb,

But then I wouldn't be the me that
   You fell in love with and
We wouldn't be what makes us,
   Us.

Somehow, you find a way
   To pick up the pieces
I couldn't piece back on my own,
   And you fill my cracks with gold,
Placing feeling back into my blank
spaces.

I know you said you'd marry me,
   But I didn't know that meant
You'd marry my pieces everyday.

## Simple Reminders

Reaching over to hold your hand in the car,

Folding your clothes,

Running my fingers up the back of your neck,

Placing your things back where they belong,

Whispering, "I love you" in your ear,

Planning for two meals instead of one,

Saying your name knowing
  It's my favorite name to say...

All simple reminders
  Of how much more me I am with you.

<u>Exhale</u>

Kissing you down your neck,
  Across your collarbone
As my fingers glide between your thighs.

You exhale in my ear,
  "Baby."

Do you know what that does to me?

## Yours

Have your way with every inch of me.

I don't want any part of me to go
  Without you being there.

Grip my neck
  And tell me I'm yours.

It's yours,

You know it's yours.

## Best View

I would follow you anywhere,
  You are my most beautiful view.

I was never a follower,
  Always going my own way,

But you,
  You placed a fork in my road,
Detouring my path.

You grabbed my hand,
  And we went running...

On the road less traveled,
  Taking the scenic route.

What a journey, babe.

Anywhere with you,
  My best view.

## Forefront

Sometimes my brain is so heavy, baby,
   And I'm sorry I don't talk.

I'm just lost in my thoughts,

But I promise you're in the forefront.
   And amongst all of these dark
thoughts,
The thought of you
   Is always the brightest.

You are the light within me when mine is
dim.

You're all I want and all I need, baby.

## Calm

When you lay your head on my chest
   And form your body into mine,
The peace that comes over me
   Is the most beautiful calm I've ever
known.

## Good Bones

My body has provided a safe home for so
many.

It served many years of comfort and
giving,

But even the strongest foundations
  Only last so long before they begin to
wilt,
And only so much can be taken from the
inside
  Before it's left with empty halls.

Well lived in, but so tired.

I no longer had a home for myself.

Then, you stumbled across this
  Abandoned space,
Deeming it had good bones,

And together we flipped it;
  We both found home.

T-shirts

I adore when you choose my clothes over
yours.

Seeing you in my t-shirts and hoodies
  Makes me feel gooey inside.

Your hair thrown up messy,
  Fresh faced,
Wrapped in what's mine.

You're just so damn cute.

## Blink

With you, hours feel like seconds.
  No time is ever enough.

It just flashes by so quickly
  And I feel like if I blink,
We will be grey.

As much as I look forward to seeing that
day,
  I do not want to get closer to the end.

You've made life worth living.

No time could ever be enough.

If I shall go before you,
  I'll keep a place next to me in Heaven.
I'll wait for you.

Soulful

You're so soulful.

You feel like 90's R&B
  On a lazy Sunday,
Candles lit and a crisp breeze
  Coming through the screen door.

It gives me butterflies,
  Chills up my spine,
And I can feel my heart race every time.

## Soft Smile

You should always know
  Just how important you are to me,
How much I think of you,
  And that you have my whole heart.

I bet you don't realize that
  Throughout my days,
You always cross my mind and
  The most genuine, soft smile
Forms across my face.

You are so loved.

Contagious

You light up every room you walk in,

Absolutely stunning.

And your smile is so brightly contagious,
  I know I'm not the only one that sees it.

We all know God took His time on you.

I can't believe He chose me to love you.

## It Rains

When it rains it pours, my love.

Loving you is easy, but nobody said
That all of this would be easy.

Just know I'm with you;
I will always walk beside you.

So, when it rains,
Let's dance in it.
Kiss me in the downpour
As the tears and raindrops
Become one on our cheeks.

We will weather all storms
As one, my love.

## Hug Me

I love when you tilt your head to the side
　And give me that little half smile that
you do
Before you melt into me and
　Lay your head on my shoulder
As I wrap my arms around you
　And kiss your head.

Don't you ever let go.
　Always hug me until I smell like you.

## Securely

I've always thrived in safety,
 I think we all do.
It's something we crave,
 Yet so hard to come by,
So we try to create it
 With every defense mechanism within
ourselves
That sometimes we build walls so
indestructible,
 Love cannot get in.

I didn't think I could let you in let alone
love,
 But you waited patiently outside my
door
Until I welcomed you inside.
 And then you took my hand,
Reassured me I was safe to come with
you,
 And we took baby steps
Until we fell so securely in love.

Thank you for keeping me safe.

## Holy Grail

I vow to love you
  In every love language there is to know
And to discover new ones you realized
you needed
  And love you in ways
I never have.

To love you better will always be my holy
grail,
  A continuous scripture
I want to learn and live by.

## Look Up

So many nights I stared into my phone
screen
  Just trying to pass the time.

And then I stared into these pages
  To love you before I had you,
Manifesting us into my life.

Everyday I'm so grateful
  To have something that
Makes me forget to look at my phone.

You are the most wonderful distraction
  From the world we live in.

This love allows me to look up.

Core

Sometimes I feel like as you shed your
layers
    You're expecting me to love you less
With the more I see,
    But I can promise you it's the opposite.

Not one part of you scares me.

Nothing about you could ever be too
much,
    You are just right for me.

I adore you and all your crazy,
    Right down to your core.

Eternally

If something should ever happen to me,
  I want you to cling onto this book
And immerse yourself in these pages.

You will hear my voice as you read,
  And I bet if you close your eyes,
You'll feel me with you.

You will never go without knowing
  You were my whole heart.

When one of us goes,
  A piece is left with the other.

You have me eternally.

I love you so much.

<u>Legacy</u>

Imagine years down the line
  When we are able to look back on
The legacy we've created.

All because two people chose to keep at it
  When love came running.

I bet our story will inspire others,

They will look at us in admiration
  For keeping old school love in this
Seemingly loveless world.

I can't wait to look at you then
  And know I got to love you that long.

Weak

It feels so good when you kiss me
  And I begin to feel your lips parting
more
As your tongue slowly slides across my
lips.

Our bodies begin to grind
  And I moan in your mouth
As I feel you go inside.

You grip me up,
  Telling me, "This is mine."
And it makes me weak every time.

Push

I know when you push me away
    You're trying to see if I'll respect your
boundaries
But still come wait for you to let me back
in.

And I know you know that I always will.

But I know it's reassuring for me to keep
coming back
    In all of those moments.

You know I'm right here, baby,
    And when push comes to shove,
I'll still be right here.

We can do that dance for however long it
takes
    To heal that part of your heart that's so
used
To love leaving.

<u>Vibe</u>

You're so fine,
  And that bad lil' vibe of yours just adds
to it.

The way you dress,
  How you speak,
The way you move...

So fine.

I look over at you and bite my lip,
  "That's mine."

## Thirsting

It's in your eyes,
    The way your lids are low and
You stare directly into my soul
    With a crave and desire
No one has ever shown me before.

One look and I'm locked in,
    Ready to give you exactly what
You're thirsting for.

My little nympho,

Have your way with me.

Get to You

And still,
  I'd do it all again
If it meant I'd get to you.

I'd go through hell,
  Walk through fire,
Cross oceans,
  Scale the greatest heights,

Any and all of it,
  A billion times over,

Just to get to you.

<u>I Do</u>

To hear you say those words,

"I do."

I do too,
  A million times over,
I do too.

## Worship

Your body is a temple,
  And I'm just here to worship.

Let me latch onto you
  And praise you with my lips.

Every part of you is divine
  And light gleams from your scars.

Glory be
  To God's perfect design
In the flesh of
  My wife.

Naked

Come out of hiding,

Show me your naked soul.

Strip down and come running to me.

I'll always have arms wide open,
    Ready to receive you intimately.

You're safe here with me.

Vessel

I needed you.

Behind this hard exterior
  Is a feminine that desperately needed
softened
By a love so gracious and relentless
  That she believed it wasn't only her
That embodied the love of God for
another human.

And you showed me that someone would
  Hit their knees for me before and after
the blessing,
Not just when the light is felt,
  But in the dark when only faith can
guide you home.

My angel on earth,
  A vessel to heaven,
I needed you.

The Chance

You're a dream.

I simply cannot comprehend
    How anyone that had a chance with
you
Didn't hold on for dear life and do all
they could
    To love you right.

But I thank them
    Because if it weren't for their failures,
I wouldn't have the chance to love you,
    And that is a chance I refuse to ever
lose.

I will spend the rest of my life
    Loving you in the ways you had always
deserved
And more.

## Constellation

Your beauty is vast,
　Like a thousand galaxies,
And stars show through your cracks
　Where you believe flaws reside.

I get lost gazing,
　Finding beauty in your creation.

Can you feel me loving you with my
eyes?

I'll still tell you because I know
　You crave to hear me admit it.

And as you watch it roll off my lips,
　You lick yours,

Awakening my bones,
　Defying my gravity.

You are my perfect constellation,
　Taking me above and beyond.

## High

My eyes were tightly shut,
  Breath deeply held,
As my lungs had the smallest capacity
  To breathe in
One
  More
Person...

And then it happened,
  This love overwhelmed my soul
And I couldn't seem to get enough.

So, I opened my eyes
  And took a hit.

Inhale,
  Exhale.

Feeling you consume my chest,
  Tingling my whole nervous system...

You are the best high I've ever felt.

Ascending

Let me take you higher,
    And we can look down on the world
As if it's ours.

Deep inside of you
    As your eyes roll back
While I set your soul on fire,
    Ascending through dimensions.

I'll grab your face
    And kiss your salt tainted lips
As you gasp in my mouth.

Let me take you there;
    Come with me.

## Fell

You are an act of faith.

When I first fell in love with you,
  Fear consumed me
And I fell to my knees and prayed.

And in that moment,
  I surrendered.

I surrendered to the risk
  And allowed my head to go over my
heels
In hopes that you'd catch me...

Or catch up to me,

And you did.

The floor gave out under our feet
  And together we flew.

## Receptors

I swear there have to be tiny receptors
  On our skin that connect our flesh
To a depth of oneness.

Our hands fold so perfectly,
  It's hard to feel that there's really any
space between them
As our heartbeats somehow begin to
pulsate as one.

I can feel your blood
  Rushing through your hands
And I swear it makes contact with my
veins,

Flowing through one another
  In perfect completion.

Calling

Before I met you
  I was so exhausted.

This journey was so trying,
  But there was this voice...

"Baby, you're almost home."
  "Please don't quit now."

And it had to be your soul speaking to
mine

Because it's the only thing
  That kept me going.

I felt you calling me home.

I'm so happy I didn't give up.

## Close as Skin

I think I'll always miss you.

I had to miss you for so long in the
waiting
  That now, I even miss you when we
sleep,
When you're in the other room,
  When we are at work,
When you're just a little too far away in
the middle of the night.

But you're always there to hold me
  As soon as you see it in my eyes
Or feel my hand reach for yours.

Now, you're as close as skin
  And I don't have to miss you for long.

## Language

I've never felt like I fit in much.
  I've always felt like the black sheep,
The oddball out,
  Not quite understood.

But you,
  You speak my language.

You recite me like a prayer
  That kept you safe
Before you laid yourself to sleep.

You
  Know
Me.

And you believe in me.

You see me in your wildest dreams,

You
  Love
Me.

## Quiet Years

As life begins to slow down,
  I look forward to each simple day
Spent with you.

We are older now,
  And in these quiet years
I am constantly reminded of
  My blessing in choosing you
And in you choosing me right back.

I can't imagine how loud the silence
would be
  If you weren't here with me.

I am so thankful for
  The sound of you.

Intergalactic

This world was never made for me.

I have always felt a part of me in a
different dimension,
    As if my soul is intergalactic.

But you make this place more digestible,
    More of a home than a floating rock
That my flesh holds my spirit hostage
on.

You fill this space with purpose,
    And if I have to exist here,
I am happy it's with you.

<u>Laced</u>

They say as we age,
  Life takes the glimmer from our eyes,

But I swear mine light up when I look at
you,
  Just like a bright-eyed kid.

And I promise when I look into yours,
  It's as if they are laced with the stars.

Life isn't taking it all from us, baby.

We will always radiate together.

## Luring

Your figure is stunning.

The candlelight casts a glow on your
frame,
   Giving my eyes the pleasure of you
While my hands already know exactly
where to go.

The rise and fall of your chest is luring,

And your breath is shallow through
parted lips.

I press mine on your forehead
   And the salt crystalizes to our skin.

I cannot comprehend how perfect you
are.

## Free Falling

I fell in love with you slowly,
   Yet all at once.

I knew once I felt that fleeting feeling,
   I was beginning my trust fall.

There was no turning back,
   There still isn't.

I wouldn't want there to be.

Luckily, we went soaring backwards
   Together
To never be caught.

We're still falling,
   Infinitely free falling.

## The Depths

In the depths and in the shallows,

Find me.

We aren't meant to tread alone,
  And you never have to now.

Even if you feel yourself going under,
  I will take a deep breath with you
And kiss you there.

<u>Family</u>

The family I have in you
  Is more than I could ever ask for,

And if this is all it ever is,
  That will be more than enough for me.

But...

If we should add tiny toes,
  Or maybe they will be tiny paws,
Or both...

Whatever it may be,
  I cannot even imagine the love that will
consume me.

What is part of you, is part of me
  And whatever we create will always be
the better part of me,
The part I look after the most.

<u>Only One</u>

Everyday you remind me of
  Exactly why it is you.

Now, you are the only woman I'll ever
love.

It will never be anyone but you
  And if it's not you, it's not anyone.

It will always be you.

I waited long enough to know,
  You are the only one.

## Ashes

I don't want to love you with the same
ordinary promises
  That the rest of the world makes.

I want to love you extraordinarily
  And far beyond human capacity.

"Till death do us part."

Yes, but further.

I want my bones curled up with yours
  In the death of our vessels.

And if I should turn to dust,
  I want my ashes as one with yours.

The last of this body begins and ends
with you.

I love you eternally.

## Any Version

What a statement...

"I do."

Do people really know what they are
agreeing to?

I know I do.

I'm gonna love you.

The woman I'm agreeing to love today
    And any version of you that you
become,

You will find me doing all I can
    To love you and her.

You are perfect for me
    Just the way you are
And she is too.

## Prove

I used to want to prove that
  True love is real
By loving women harder than they loved
me.

Unintentional but destructible...

The only place that got me was
  Needing the same type of saving

And I thought I'd never get it,

That maybe something was wrong with
me
  And the way I love.

Then you showed up
  And you kept coming for me.

Every time I expected you to go,
  You were standing right there waiting.

Sometimes I still have to rub my eyes
  To make sure I'm not dreaming.

## Deeper

Your back deeply arches as
  I drift my palms down your spine,
Pushing your chest further into the
mattress.

I press deeper
  As your soft sighs almost beg me to
stop,
But I know that means you want more.

This is the only place I'll hurt you...

And I'll make it feel so good.

## Enamored

Sometimes when you're sleeping
  I trace your face,
Running my fingers from your forehead,
  Down your jawline,
And back to your earlobes.

It is one of my most favorite intimate
moments
  That we share, and the best part is
That you don't even know we're having
it.

Don't you ever worry your pretty little
mind,

I am enamored of you.

## Indulge

From the first time
   I experienced the taste of you,
I knew I was hooked.

It's as if all parts of you
   Were made for my tongue to indulge

And I simply
   Cant
Get
   Enough.

I crave you so intensely.

There is a burning desire within my
chest
   And my stomach flutters at the
thought,

So much so
   That I still taste you on my lips.

## Fluent

The way we know one another in the
dark
  Is poetic.

We are so fluent in one another
  That the shadows do not obscure our
vision.

Rather, this is the place we see one
another so clearly...

Nude
  Messy
Tangled into one.

Permanent

I now understand why love felt so
temporary
  In my past.

And while that hurt,
  I became so convinced and settled into
the concept.

It felt so uncomfortable being so
comfortable
  With the art of detachment.

But now, I understand.

It will all feel as such until
  The other half of your soul arrives
To carry the weight of love, making it

Light
  Airy
Permanent.

## White

And so
  We both wore white,

In our auras
  And these gowns

Clean
  Pure
Innocent

But so intentional and powerful,
  Exactly how love should be.

And we devoted ourselves to a Godly
union

Until we exit this place...

And again, we will wear white
  As we enter eternity
As one.

## Under Moonlight

Darkness is a tricky place.
   There is beauty in it,
Yet it is home to so many things we fear.

With you
   Not so much.

It is the place we share our deepest
secrets
   And reveal the most intimate parts of
Our flesh and bones.

We always utilize our time while the sun
is at rest,
   Kissing under moonlight.

## Listen

I know you were left empty one too many
times
   And I promise you didn't deserve that.

I wish I could have got to you sooner
   So that love would spare you some
hurt,

But I'm here now.

I'm all yours
   And I'll listen to all that you lost
And replace it all
   With what stays.

I can't promise that I can fix it,
   But I promise you can rest in these
arms while
I listen.

## Cohesive

And finally...
  For once,
I met the right woman at the right time.

This is seamless, just right,
  Effortless.

The river that flows in you flows in me
too.

Our gravity creates an infinite current
  To not be disrupted.

These bodies are cohesive,
  A unit in love's legacy.

## Just Kiss Me

If you're ever unsure of what to do with
me,
   Just kiss me.

This mind is my worst enemy
   And sometimes that's debilitating,

But there's nothing that can silence the
thoughts
   Like the power within your lips pressed
against mine.

Grab my face
   And just kiss me
In the way that you would if
   Our lungs were inhaling for the final
time.

## Homeward

The days won't always be easy, baby.

I can't promise that it won't rain;
  I can't keep that away,

But I will be your shelter.

Haul off and come running to me

And I'll make you laugh
  While I wipe the tears that fell
As we watch the rest dry.

I'll always try my best to be
  Who you need me to be,

Especially when you're looking
homeward.

## Boundless

No words could ever be enough.

Thoughts and heart
  Poured to paper,
Yet there could never be enough ink.

I love you more now than I ever have
  And way less than I will tomorrow.

The way I feel for you is boundless,
  But if you should ever worry,

Fall into these pages
  And let me remind you
That I love being yours,

All yours.

# About the Author

# Leah Maurizio

Leah Maurizio is a poet from Pittsburgh, Pennsylvania. She first discovered her love for writing poetry in 8th grade and incorporated creative writing classes into her high school electives at Shaler Area High School. In addition, Leah is also a Hip Hop dancer and choreographer, specializing in training the youth. She began dancing Hip Hop at the age of 8, which has been her main passion ever since. Upon graduation from Point Park University's Rowland School of Business in 2016, she decided to follow her heart and continue to pursue her dancing career. This career took a turn during the 2019 pandemic, which motivated Leah to go back to school in 2021 to become an esthetician. She now juggles both careers full time.

Outside of the spa and studio, Leah values being with her family and small circle of friends. She believes heavily in love being the most powerful thing in the world and aims to always lead with it. She currently resides with her dog and best friend, Glizzy, in the North Hills of Pittsburgh.

As a lesbian, she is a proud member of the LGBTQIA+ community, always advocating and striving for representation. It is very important to her to aid in the success of equality, sexual orientation normalization, and being a role model to the youth. This is her first poetry book, which exemplifies lesbian love and representation.

If you wish to follow along her journey, you can find her on social media, @leahmaurizio.

Made in the USA
Middletown, DE
17 May 2025

75624394R00078